# SPINE-CHILLERS 2021

## SPOOKTACULAR TALES

Edited By Roseanna Caswell

First published in Great Britain in 2021 by:

 Young**Writers**®
Est. 1991

Young Writers
Remus House
Coltsfoot Drive
Peterborough
PE2 9BF
Telephone: 01733 890066
Website: www.youngwriters.co.uk

Printed and bound in the UK by BookPrintingUK
Website: www.bookprintinguk.com
YB0487O

# FORELUORD

Enter, Reader, if you dare...

For as long as there have been stories there have been ghost stories. Writers have been trying scare their readers for centuries using just the power of their imagination. For Young Writers' latest competition Spine-Chillers we asked pupils to come up with their own spooky tales, but with the tricky twist of using just 100 words!

They rose to the challenge magnificently and this resulting collection of haunting tales will certainly give you the creeps! From friendly ghosts and Halloween adventures to the gruesome and macabre, the young writers in this anthology showcase their creative writing talents.

Here at Young Writers our aim is to encourage creativity and to inspire a love of the written word, so it's great to get such an amazing response, with some absolutely fantastic stories.

I'd like to congratulate all the young authors in this collection - I hope this inspires them to continue with their creative writing. And who knows, maybe we'll be seeing their names alongside Stephen King on the best seller lists in the future...

# CONTENTS

## St Paul's Way Trust School, Tower Hamlets

| | |
|---|---|
| Eris Hoxha (12) | 35 |
| Summer Roberts (12) | 36 |
| Muhammed Rahman (12) | 37 |
| Irene Jaques (12) | 38 |
| Daniel Lopez Mercado (12) | 39 |

## St Richard's Catholic College, Bexhill-On-Sea

| | |
|---|---|
| Elise Kennedy (15) | 40 |
| Christie Winthe (12) | 41 |
| Henry Kicinski-Mason (12) | 42 |
| Olivia Mathew (15) | 43 |
| May Fogarty-Stevens (15) | 44 |
| Jed Bayjou-Bates (12) | 45 |
| Sebastian Button (12) | 46 |
| Glen Bracken (13) | 47 |
| Harry Rouse (13) | 48 |
| Besiana Martinaj (14) | 49 |
| Renisse Gregorio (13) | 50 |
| Finley Hide (13) | 51 |
| Ivy Weeks-Pearson (13) | 52 |
| Zoe Pisani-Cleland (15) | 53 |
| Carla Herring (12) | 54 |
| Rory Eade (16) | 55 |
| Jessica Cart (11) | 56 |

## Staffordshire University Academy, Hednesford

| | |
|---|---|
| Seth Tomes (13) | 57 |
| Dominic Jones (12) | 58 |
| Sam Stanton (14) | 59 |
| Mason Whittingham (13) | 60 |
| Molly Duffy (13) | 61 |
| Izzy Brown-Jones (13) | 62 |
| Mia Collins-Hodgetts (12) | 63 |
| Seth Gray (13) | 64 |
| Alex Corns (12) | 65 |
| Jack Robinson (13) | 66 |
| Lilly Gooch (13) | 67 |

| | |
|---|---|
| Jack Dunne (13) | 68 |
| Danielle Morning (13) | 69 |
| Eva Hopkins (13) | 70 |
| Chloe Harrison (13) | 71 |
| Harvey Duke (12) | 72 |
| Chloe Julian (13) | 73 |
| Nathan Collins (14) | 74 |
| Shannon Tomkinson (13) | 75 |
| Finlay Hull (12) | 76 |
| Charlie Brockhurst (14) | 77 |

## Suffolk One, Pinewood

| | |
|---|---|
| Poppy Lacey (17) | 78 |

## Swanmore College, Swanmore

| | |
|---|---|
| Alice Dibb (13) | 79 |
| Lillie Vivian (14) | 80 |
| Chloe Harvey | 81 |
| Archie C (12) | 82 |
| Sophie Smith (12) | 83 |

## Sydney Russell School, Dagenham

| | |
|---|---|
| Elisa Gjoka (13) | 84 |
| Ruth Ogbuokiri (13) | 85 |

## The Beacon Centre, South Shields

| | |
|---|---|
| Kieron Batey (14) | 86 |
| Faith Brown (13) | 87 |
| Callum Fontaine (12) | 88 |

## The Gateway Academy, Tilbury

| | |
|---|---|
| Paige Whittaker (15) | 89 |

## The Henrietta Barnett School, Hampstead Garden Suburb

| | |
|---|---|
| Gia Bhalla (12) | 90 |
| Hannah Boolaky (12) | 91 |

Aishwarya Kozhikkottu
Mundakkaparambil (13) — 92
Sofia Kountouri (12) — 93

## The Magna Carta School, Staines-Upon-Thames

| | |
|---|---|
| Calin Neagu. (12) | 94 |
| Joshua Makepeace (12) | 95 |
| James Burdett (12) | 96 |
| Iona Ogilvie (12) | 97 |
| Ollie Bailey | 98 |
| Megan Young (12) | 99 |
| Maeve Parkin (12) | 100 |
| Milly Clark (12) | 101 |
| Nadia Swierczynska (12) | 102 |
| Ilke Savas (12) | 103 |
| Seth Fisher (11) | 104 |
| Ethan Woods (12) | 105 |
| Adam Hiley (12) | 106 |
| Dhiyana Padmanabhan (12) | 107 |
| Charlie Cotsworth (12) | 108 |
| Jemimah Ahmed (13) | 109 |
| Tanya Kawenya (12) | 110 |
| Luke Balaam (12) | 111 |
| Summer Digby (11) | 112 |
| Chloe Wells | 113 |
| Dylan Rodriguez (12) | 114 |

## The Quay School, Parkstone

| | |
|---|---|
| Zoe Thorne (15) | 115 |
| Amy Heyward-Allen (16) | 116 |
| Jacob Thompson (15) | 117 |
| Alfie Lambert (15) | 118 |

## The Stanway School, Stanway

| | |
|---|---|
| Sophie Pasfield (12) | 119 |
| Finlay Panther | 120 |

## Trinity Academy Grammar, Sowerby Bridge

| | |
|---|---|
| Haaris Sarwar (12) | 121 |
| Annabel Walker (13) | 122 |
| Kamran Azam (13) | 123 |
| Lalith Togalla (13) | 124 |
| Corbin Taylor (14) | 125 |
| Lily Roberts (13) | 126 |
| Malachy Burns (15) | 127 |
| Nimrah Nabeel (12) | 128 |
| Sophie Calder (13) | 129 |

## Workington Academy, Workington

| | |
|---|---|
| Josh Torney (14) | 130 |
| Acacia McLean (14) | 131 |
| Jayden Messenger (14) | 132 |
| Lilly Fidoe (12) | 133 |
| Preston Keeler (14) | 134 |
| Riley McLuckie (14) | 135 |
| Archie Mahone | 136 |
| Daniel Weightman (12) | 137 |
| Owain Graham (14) | 138 |
| Niamh McNicholas (12) | 139 |
| Riley Underwood (12) | 140 |
| Chloe Ellwood (14) | 141 |

# THE MINI SAGAS

# THE INTRUDER

My conscience shifted back to reality. The man had checked the whole house, or so he thought.

I felt for a moment as if I was the only person in the world and everyone wanted to kill me. This man, this crazed man could actually do it. Insane laughter broke out, echoing around the room.

The floorboards creaked, dust rising from the ground like cancerous smoke, approaching, choking me.

My breath shook and my heart pounded, the lines of light, shadowed on my face, faded as my hope and my final moments slowly dissolved. Growing darker and darker. Pitch-black. Nothingness.

**Ryan Fairhurst (17)**
Petroc College, Barnstaple

# HALLOWEEN FROM HELL

One stormy October night, Luke was watching spooky films to fit the mood. He was suddenly disturbed by a startling loud bang on his front door. It was a young girl, merely ten years old. She was pale and bony, almost skeleton-like. It was strange that this would happen at 3am but he let her inside anyway. However, as soon as they were both inside, the front door slammed shut and all the lights turned off! He couldn't find the girl! No sign of her anywhere! When he turned around, he realised, it was not a little girl at all...

**Bethany Northover (17)**
Petroc College, Barnstaple

# THE HOUSE

Georgie slowly opened the door, letting out the cries of a ghost.

"Come on, Kelly," she said, tilting her head towards the house. "It'll be fun!"

"No!" Kelly replied, "I'm not going!"

Georgie shrugged and proceeded to enter.

The creepy house was dark and scary, but Georgie carried on.

After exploring around, Georgie noticed an urn, all clean and shiny. She decided to open it. Suddenly, she started to shrink. She shrunk to the size where she was small enough to fit inside.

"Georgie!" Kelly yelled.

"Kelly! Please... save me!" Georgie cried, before disappearing into the urn.

## Callista Msulira (13)
Plymouth College, Plymouth

# NOTHING BENEATH IT

"Tracey, follow me," whispered Caroline.
*Drip!* The thick sticky black substance fell from the mouldy roof. What felt like a ghost brushed past Caroline's shoulder. Stumbling further and further into the tunnel, their hands in front of them, they felt a jagged rock-shaped circle. Caroline flicked her torch on with her trembling fingers, blue like the ocean. It revealed a never-ending well, as dark as the night.
"Watch out, Caroline! Don't lean too far in," Tracey said cautiously.
The light flickered. They dropped a rock and waited for a splash but nothing was there nothing beneath it.

**Freya Pearson (13)**
Plymouth College, Plymouth

# KNOCK! KNOCK!

*Knock! Knock!*
My spine shivered.
*Knock! Knock!*
I heard a chainsaw, blood splattered on the window, broken glass everywhere. I hid. The screaming pierced my ears. I had a chance to escape.
I sprinted to the nearest house banging on the door. A slender body opened the creaking door.
"Hello," he said, "are you okay?"
I tried to scream but the words weren't coming out. I broke into a panic. I heard the chainsaw coming for me. I blacked out.
I woke up in an asylum.
"Don't worry, this won't hurt too much..."
"Argh!"

## Sonny Leigh (13)
Plymouth College, Plymouth

# REBECCA

There was ferocious rain crashing against the windows. The wind was howling like a wolf trying to find its parents. Rebecca sat in the corner of the gloomy room with a candle in her hand, watching the water slide down the partly cracked windows. She could hear the floorboards creaking. She tried to get to sleep but she couldn't. She could hear voices outside.

"Rebecca, get to sleep!" shouted her parents.

Rebecca replied nervously, "I can't. All I can hear is the wind howling and the wind crashing against the windows. There are people here too..."

**Ollie Heath (13)**
Plymouth College, Plymouth

# UNFITTING

The day when the night was not so bright, was also the day when the monsters came to fright.

"Jess, come here," she shouted as the TV went dark.

"What's the matter?" she slurred.

*Bang!* The floorboards creaked loudly and a black substance came rising slowly out of the cracks like the devil crawling out of hell. The light brown floorboards quickly became black. It started walking up the walls. The black substance looked smooth and silky, almost like water. Then it slowly started running up the ceiling right above Sarah...

**Joseph Bibby (12)**
Plymouth College, Plymouth

# SILENCE

"Otto, come on. If we leave now we can make it home before nightfall. This place is giving me the creeps."
"You have been reading too many horror novels. We will be fine."
All around the barren landscape, there was no escape. The dilapidated house loomed over us like a tiger watching its prey. The house gave us a sense of mystery. A letter lay on the doorstep saying: 'You will suffer'. We decided to lock the door just in case of the worst.
At 2am we heard a noise. The door opened but there was silence...

## Harry Godefroy (13)
Plymouth College, Plymouth

# IT WAS ME?

As I inched towards the black rusted chamber, I felt my hands start to quake as I hovered my fingertips over the coarse metal handle. An ear-piercing scream scraped my soul, as I tore open the tiniest crack of the fallen door.
I slid into the endless darkness, stifling my desire to let out a cry. All I heard was the dying rats high on poison. My eyes fell upon one single decayed casket. Then another and another. The door slammed shut. I flung my body around. Someone was with me. I could hear them panting. My secret was out...

## Lilly Whittingham (13)
Plymouth College, Plymouth

# THE SPIRIT

The screaming and squealing of the wind in the graveyard rang in my ears. Lurking mist glided over the tombstones. I glanced up and got a glimpse of a shadow dancing around a grave. It seemed like it was encroaching on my position. I trembled, palms sweaty. I still didn't know what I was looking at but it was staring at me intensely, angrily, furiously. His small frame made me think it was a child. His hands and feet were so big but his arms were so small. It finally arrived; it was a spirit that had unfinished business.

**Felix Builder (14)**
Plymouth College, Plymouth

# WANTED

I looked up at the wet, soggy piece of paper which had my face on it. Imprinted underneath were the haunted letters: 'Wanted'.
They were after me and there was nothing I could do. Why? After all the pain and suffering I fought through, I, of all people, had to be blamed and punished for crimes I had not committed. I hid my tears as the daunting drops of rain came plummeting down on me as if I was sinking into the deserted concrete below me. Then I heard the deafening sound of sirens. It was over. I'm done...

## Ethan Jefford (13)
Plymouth College, Plymouth

# THE CRIME OF PASSION

Slipping on my new white gloves, we started to walk slowly down the dusty cobbled staircase. We crept into the darkness, my partner not knowing what he had gotten himself into.

Clear light flickered on. Revealing the shiny silver knife I held in my hand. He knew at that moment what was going to happen. And for the last time, we stared into each other's eyes which showed all the guilt and fear we held.

The lights flickered off and I walked back up the stairs into the light, removing my red bloodstained gloves.

**Olivia Grundy (13)**
Plymouth College, Plymouth

# BELOW DECKS

The cold steel walls creaked like a tree standing in strong winds. I waded through the icy cold water and ran up the rusted stairs. I struggled to open the metal gate. I was trapped.

All of a sudden, the lights turned dark and I froze in fear. There was no escape from this slowly filling prison.

The water had now reached my hips and I could no longer feel my feet. At this point, I had given up all hope. I thought I was going to drown now rather than later because I'd been too long underwater.

## Joel Witherall (13)
Plymouth College, Plymouth

# THE CLOWN?

I had a shiver down my spine when I saw the pitch-black night at 3am. There was a red kind of figure in the distance of my McDonald's. I thought it might be Ronald McDonald, the clown, but as I got closer, the figure got clearer and clearer. It didn't look like Ronald McDonald any more.
It got scarier and scarier. It started to move towards me like it was teleporting. Because it was so fast, I couldn't see it any more. Then I felt something breathing heavily behind me...

**Archie Innes (13)**
Plymouth College, Plymouth

# HIM

Darkness, total darkness. Darkness invaded the glowing, gleaming, glaring light high up in the stygian sky, a cannonball of deadly fire. The sun's heavenly splendour, accompanied by its troop of scintillating stars, was a shining circle of good submerged in the demonic, dooming darkness. Could this be the place he meant?
Beneath the Brobdingnagian trees' sharp, pointed fingers (which seemingly ceased the moon), lifelessly lay the dying bodies of once towering, tormenting trees. This was it.
Death entered my skin like a moth attacking a shroud. As I sunk to the ground, his silhouette arose.

## Lwle Preston Yates (14)
Queen Ethelburga's College, York

# TO DREAM OR NOT TO DREAM?

Blood dripped from its mouth. I could feel its eyes staring into my soul through the window. It was about to break the glass, although I knew it couldn't come in without my permission.

*Crack!*

I woke up screaming. I was in a pool of cold sweat. There was a knock on my door.

My mum's voice said, "I heard you screaming, can I come in?"

Relieved, I said, "Yes. I've just had an awful dream, Mum."

Then, with cold dread, I realised that I'd left for college three weeks ago and that I'd just let that vile thing in...

## Izzy Harkness (12)
Queen Margaret's School, Escrick

# LURKING IN THE CHURCH

On a dark, misty night, I heard the church clock chime. The handle of the door was rusty but unlocked.
The door creaked open and a gust of wind pushed me through it. *Bang!* The door slammed shut!
"Hello?"
No answer. I tiptoed up the aisle and stood at the lectern. I stared down at the bible. On it was a message written in red lipstick. It read: 'I am here!'
Suddenly, I heard a scream. There was a warm, harsh breath on my back. Blood was dripping everywhere. I looked up and saw two eyes glaring down at me...

## Camilla Eliis (12)
Queen Margaret's School, Escrick

# THE UNKNOWN

It was behind me. Following me. Watching me. I could feel its presence, forcing me towards the door. And it wasn't taking no for an answer. Fighting against it, I tried to push myself away from the door, but as I did, the doorknob turned, and the door shifted open.

Subconsciously, I began to walk through the doors of the abandoned, immense manor. Already regretting my decision, the door slammed shut, the windows clattered to a close, the street lights began to flicker and I was left alone. Alone with my thoughts. Alone with its presence... Just me and them...

## Kayleigh Silk (14)
Redhill School & Specialist Language College, Stourbridge

# I FOUND YOU!

I don't think that the world's split into good and bad, but as I stare at the words on the paper, I doubted myself. 'I found you'.

Trembling, my eyes skimmed over the letters again. Slowly, I turned, facing the dark corridor. My breath caught as I saw him. His features were almost entirely concealed by shadows, but I'll never be able to escape that face. He has come for me.

I don't think that the world's split into good and bad, but as I stared into the eyes of the man that I murdered, I began to doubt myself.

## Rebecca Pierce (12)
South Craven School, Cross Hills

# I LIVE ALONE...

June 6th, 2006. My birthday. I had woken abruptly to the sound of a raging thunderstorm. Thunder rumbled ominously before crashing and howling overhead. As a guillotine blade of lightning streaked across the horizon, it illuminated a peculiarly wrapped package, which had been precariously placed on my desk. I didn't recall who I had received this from.

As I unwrapped the package, there was another colossal rumble of thunder. Inside was a small camera, despite my uninterest in photography. I looked at the library; there was a picture of me sleeping, taken on 6th June 2006.

I live alone...

**Imaan Khan (12)**
St Albans High School For Girls, St. Albans

# SCREAMING CRIMSON

Crimson stood at the dwelling. She could turn back. She knew this. But it felt like a magnet was pulling her forward. The draught was brushing against her porcelain face. Her caramel eyes fluttered with anxiety. Her fingers crinkled from the cold. She went in. She pushed the creaking door open, disturbing the eerie, tangible silence in the house. It was gargantuan and, against her instinct, she climbed the stairs. Something was wrong. Her black hair seemed to spread around her rotund head. Her feet seemed to float. Her heart raced. Something brushed her shoulder. She turned around. She screamed.

## Naima Mohib (12)
St Albans High School For Girls, St. Albans

# THE PACKAGE

*Ding-dong!* The storm scraped at my house. *Ding-dong!* I creaked open the door and froze. A pale man with a wide, toothy smile was standing there, dripping and staring straight back at me. He slowly handed me a package tied with brown paper and red string. I took it indoors, opened it and reeled back, retching. It was a human toe.
The next day, I woke up to searing pain, already dreading what it was. My big toe was gone. It kept happening. Fingers, an eye, even hair.
Today, I received a new package. It was a tongue...

## Rosan Trisic (14)
St Albans High School For Girls, St. Albans

# BEEP!

I decided to take a break from the city and rented a house in the countryside. I left all my electronics in the city too. It was already dark, so I went to sleep. Suddenly, I heard *beep! Beep!* I looked out of the window but the garden was empty.

Slowly, I fell back asleep. *Beep! Beep!* A tall, skinny, mechanical being crashed through the window and landed at the foot of my bed in a shower of glass. I froze. The thing looked me straight in the eye, growled, flexed its claws and then inched forward...

## Esrom Andom (14)

St Illtyd's Catholic High School, Rumney

# THE TITANS

My five friends and I went biking late at night in a shady dense forest. It was rather cold and misty. Everything was going fine. In fact, my friends and I were having the time of our lives, until we heard a hostile whistle coming from the trees.

All of a sudden, giant, human-like Titans ambushed us and grabbed my friend, Leo. In one motion, the Titan picked him up and ate him. I stood, frozen to the ground and watched as my friend's body was squashed and mangled between the Titan's teeth. I turned and ran...

**Damon Bellington (14)**
St Illtyd's Catholic High School, Rumney

# THING

It was cold, dark and gloomy. I could barely see. All I could hear were branches snapping and the wind howling. Suddenly, I heard laughter. A sinister noise filled with hatred. Then I saw it!

I ran as quickly as I could, dodging trees and ditches. I could hear giant steps behind me, close to me. I could see a streetlamp and a road in front of me. I sprinted forwards. Just as my foot hit the tarmac, I felt a sharp claw on my leg. I fell and turned to see purple, angry eyes inches from my face...

## Callum Jones (14)
St Illtyd's Catholic High School, Rumney

# THE PLAGUE DOCTOR

My friends and I went into the woods. We heard rustling in the trees behind us. We didn't think anything of it until a tall figure approached us. As the light hit him, we realised he was dressed like a plague doctor. He didn't see us as he passed, so we followed him.
He led us to a house in the middle of nowhere. There were children in cages. Some were dead and others malnourished, looking like they were on the brink of extinction. He took off his mask and I saw my dad's face!

## Callum Wales (14)

St Illtyd's Catholic High School, Rumney

# THE GIRL

One day, my friend, Tyler, and I were walking in the forest. We came across an old, broken house.
We entered and immediately heard crying from the room across from us. Quietly, we crept forward. A girl stood with her back to us.
"What's wrong?"
Slowly, she lifted her head and began turning to face us. The light from a broken window shone on her face, revealing a pair of sharp, vicious fangs and an evil look on her face...

## Tommy Harrington-Riby (14)
St Illtyd's Catholic High School, Rumney

# THE GREEN GHOST

There the ghost was, right in front of Pierre's eyes.
Pierre muttered in Belgian, "Ghosts, ghosts, ghosts."
A loud shriek scarred over the sky. Pierre jumped out onto
his porch. Within moments, he was out on the road.
He saw a strange sight, ghosts, driving in cars, walking on
the road. He had known this was the village that was
bombed at this exact time; 4.48am. Were these signs
something else was going to happen?
He scrambled inside his home and found the newspaper
report with the title: 'Torgny bombed!' Would it happen
again?

**Zane Sifuna (12)**
St Michael's Catholic School, High Wycombe

# IT WAS ALL A DREAM AGAIN

*Boosh!* I forgot everything. It was like the redolence existence in me disappeared that night before waking up. I dreamt something so real, so surreal, that had happened that night.

The succeeding day, I went to work. Usually, there would be many people working at their computer stations but at that moment, no one that I could think of was lingering there. It was anomalous and a bit weird. I saw my friend.

I asked him, "Where is everyone?"

He didn't respond.

It was at that moment that I realised it was all still a dream.

## Darius Bejenaru (12)
St Michael's Catholic School, High Wycombe

# AWAKENING

Anita sat on her bed, watching the rain thundering harshly on the ground. It would only be a matter of time before she started feeling dizzy. She was right because, at that very moment, she felt her head spinning. She couldn't take it anymore.

She headed for the forest. She squinted as the shooting pains kicked in around her head. A glowing, silver pendant peeked out from under a pile of leaves. Without realising what she was doing, she put it on. A mist of darkness filled the atmosphere and all that could be heard was a loud, shrill scream.

**Fatima Chohan (12)**
St Michael's Catholic School, High Wycombe

# DARKNESS

I found myself in darkness. The last thing I could remember was being beside my mother's death bed.
Suddenly, a purple light from the sky revealed an abandoned mansion. Lightning struck one of the naked trees three metres away from the mansion.
I ran and ran, but no matter how far I travelled, the house appeared right in front of me. I was in a loop. I was certain I was in a dream until lightning struck the house. Wood everywhere. I closed my eyes and saw my mother screaming. I tried to save her but found myself in darkness.

## Tommy Murphy (12)
St Michael's Catholic School, High Wycombe

# THE ANCIENT HOUSE

The ancient house stood there. The dark windows seeped into my soul like a curse, but I was drawn to it, I couldn't stop myself.

I opened the door. My attention was immediately drawn to the chandelier. It creaked over my head, the crystals staring daggers at me. Then something caught my eye.

The candle wax was dripping over the side like a gash. Then the flame went out and everything went dark. I turned around to leave but there was someone in the doorway. They reached out and I felt my soul exiting my body and I was gone...

## William Fletcher
St Michael's Catholic School, High Wycombe

# TOGETHER ALONE

I ran far. So far that the house that I just came from looked smaller than a seed. I wanted to get away from what was making me deranged. I hated it there. Leaving was the best decision I ever made, running away for freedom.

As I swept the madness off my face and took some arbitrary turns, I realised that I was alone in the woods. It was pitch-black. The only thing I could see was the full moon. I started to feel apprehensive. The prickly trees surrounded me. Everything felt like it was watching me. I was scared.

## Camila Lukaszek (12)
St Michael's Catholic School, High Wycombe

# GOTHIC STORY

I woke up one early Sunday morning, laying in bed listening to the noises going through my head. I sat in fear, waiting for something bad to happen.

My name is Mia and I'm ten years old. Unfortunately, a few weeks ago, my mum passed away from a tumour. I live with my dad now, but he goes off to work so I don't see him much.

I don't have any friends as they all betrayed me. I feel lonely and I'm worried because if my dad dies I'll be alone. My heart raced and there was silence...

## Holly Newell-Gosling (12)
St Michael's Catholic School, High Wycombe

# EMERGENCY ALERT

It was the dead of night. I was peacefully on cloud nine, listening to blaring chimes from my phone and the motel television when I was pulled out of my serene state, abruptly.

The first thing I saw was scrolling white text on a jet-black background. 'Emergency Alert of unknown type issued for your location at request of civil authorities. Lock doors and windows, disregard any requests for entry, whether they sound human. Do not search for missing pets or relatives'. My blood ran cold as I heard a knock on the door.

"Open up! Room service here!"

## Eris Hoxha (12)
St Paul's Way Trust School, Tower Hamlets

# TWIN'S DEATH

Zac and Ryan both led a normal life; football, home, sleep, repeat. Until something changed Ryan. It was his brother, he was so much more successful and happier than him.

One night, whilst Zac was asleep, Ryan took a sharp slice of his brother's throat and hid his body in the woods near his house.

Ryan finally had everything; the grades, the leadership. No one could stop him.

In the morning, Ryan told his mum, "Zac snuck out."

Everything was perfectly planned until his twin ran back through the door. Exposing the secret they once shared...

## Summer Roberts (12)
St Paul's Way Trust School, Tower Hamlets

# THE BEGINNING OF THE DEAD REVOLUTION

In the east of London, a poor old man died at midnight. His family mourned his loss and buried him in the South Groves Cemetery.

"... dust to dust; in sure and certain hope of the Resurrection to eternal life. We mourn the loss of our friend, Zak Parker."

But then, in the middle of the night, a weird rumbling came from underneath a baby's grave. Suddenly, a dead baby's corpse jumped out. The corpse looked around and grinned. However, the grave where Zak was buried cracked open and a dead hand peeked out.

The beginning of the dead revolution...

**Muhammed Rahman (12)**
St Paul's Way Trust School, Tower Hamlets

# THE ORIANA

I crept through the silent classroom. Only moments before, her hands had been digging into my arm; her knife in my face. My hands ran over the marks Oriana had burned into me: "to ensure you don't forget me." Aurora suited her better.

A cold hand closed over my neck. I spun, kicking her in the groin. As she doubled over, I jumped to her shoulders, kicking her head. Blood streamed from it. I spent no time admiring my handiwork.

Running into the cold night of ordinary people, I was the unusual person. My face said it all.

**Irene Jaques (12)**
St Paul's Way Trust School, Tower Hamlets

# THE CHANGING ROOM

Shortly after swimming, we entered the changing room. We were met by a cold silence. Slowly, we trod over puddles, wary of the slick floor.

A pair of ocean-blue shorts floated eerily, unmoving, as if being worn by the puddle. The shorts contorted in forms so humanoid, yet almost alien. Torrents of water formed the shape of a hand and reposed under my friend's chin.

The lights returned. The hand: gone. The sheen of sweat we all wore was evidence of the nightmare. Our eyes turned to the floor; a hand-shaped puddle lay in front of us.

## Daniel Lopez Mercado (12)
St Paul's Way Trust School, Tower Hamlets

# DIRT IN THE HALLS

*Badump-badump-ba. Breath.*
"Oh, God."
In...
"Please, no!"
And out...
"Dear God, or whoever is listening."
Breathe in...
"Please not me, not today."
And out...
She breathed in one last shuddering breath. Her lungs gradually stopped inflating. Her once fast-beating heart now stopped dead in its tracks. Her limbs froze in what would be their final resting place. Her heavy, weary head lay gently with a thud on the soil and bloodstained wood...
And, if only for a second, a single heartbeat, she heard it. A noise that would be the last she ever heard. Heavy, hefty and sturdy footsteps...

## Elise Kennedy (15)
St Richard's Catholic College, Bexhill-On-Sea

# WATCH THE SHADOW

Our school is infamous for going too far on Halloween, but never as far as this year.

Miss said there was a trip to Harley's Mansion. It was haunted, so we were excited.

We played, running like it was a maze. A door slammed and the lights flickered, abruptly changing the atmosphere.

I saw an unidentifiable shadow.

A voice whispered, "Harley's following..."

"Very funny," I said, feeling uneasy.

Sensing the tension, I smiled.

A hand, so cold I shivered, pressed against my mouth, hissing, "Shush!"

I froze, paralysed. I saw its glowing red eyes.

It bellowed, "I warned you..."

## Christie Winthe (12)
St Richard's Catholic College, Bexhill-On-Sea

# DEAD BLOOD

Christmas. Chaos. Blood. It stained and dried on the ground. The night before last was the evening before Christmas. The road outside was filled with parked cars. Joey's dad was reading him a famous story.

"Not a creature was stirring, not even a mouse!" he exclaimed.

Yet, he didn't know that was true, well, nobody did. Because lurking outside the room was a man in a red suit. He seemed to look like Santa but had a knife. Dripping with blood. Did he think that it was Halloween? Maybe!

Joey looked outside, "Dad..."

His voice suddenly muffled.

"Joey?"

"Huh?"

## Henry Kicinski-Mason (12)
St Richard's Catholic College, Bexhill-On-Sea

# BURY THE BODY

"Tell me the truth!" I shouted, sobbing, gripping the knife tighter in my hand.

She looked at me blankly, wet hair draping from her scalp. Her clothes were equally as wet and her hands drenched in blood and dirt.

"Tell me you didn't do it!"

My back slowly straightened, holding me high enough to tower over her. My wrist slowly turned with each passing second, pointing the tip, towards her.

"Who were you burying in the swamp?" I asked, harsher than before.

She took a few steps towards me and whispered in my ear, "You know who..."

She cackled evilly.

## Olivia Mathew (15)
St Richard's Catholic College, Bexhill-On-Sea

# THE MONSTERS

The monsters opened the door of the nursery and coaxed you from your sheltered hiding place. Simpering, smiling voices calling softly.
Lizzy led you. Golden Lizzy, Heaven's missing angel. Lucifer was an angel. She enjoyed cruelty. She ripped the wings off butterflies and shut cats' tails in doors.
We all liked her. She made us feel like deities: untouchable. We became drunk on the fumes of her power.
It was her idea to send you down to the basement, with no candle.
I heard your screams when cobwebs ensnared you.
You opened the dumbwaiter and Crept in.
You didn't know...

## May Fogarty-Stevens (15)
St Richard's Catholic College, Bexhill-On-Sea

# THE NARROWING

A faint croaking sound emerged from the school that kept a steady rhythm, making Oscar jump regularly in startlement. The urge and fright contrasted, restricting him from entering the plain of abandoned darkness when the sight of blood cascading out the entrance, interspersed in a sudden rush as if it had been cooped up.

The crimson river, which had formed in a matter of moments, slowly trickled down to the road where Oscar's feet stood rooted. The chaos was seemingly over when out stepped a frail, cadaverous woman wearing a prominent crimson-stained gown. Then, a silence-breaking scream reverberated.

## Jed Bayjou-Bates (12)
St Richard's Catholic College, Bexhill-On-Sea

# THE TALE OF THE MURDEROUS CHILD

Strolling down a lonely path in the woods, a creepy ghost was happily humming to himself. Suddenly, a child, a small girl, dripping in blood, stepped onto the path. She must've been no older than eight.

She slowly raised her blood-coated arm and pointed at the ghost while blood drip down her sleeve. Petrified, the ghost ran, scared out of his wits.

He ran until he found a crooked house. A sign said: 'Keep out!' The ghost was too ignorant to notice it.

Walking down a spooky corridor, the ghost saw the child again. Then consciousness slowly escaped him.

## Sebastian Button (12)
St Richard's Catholic College, Bexhill-On-Sea

# THE HUNTSMAN

As you aimlessly wander through the vast unknown caves, the sounds of screaming bounce from wall to wall. Your quivering hands delicately hold a small yet vital item, a lighter, a small light source pacifies the urge to run.
You know something is out there. The only problem is you don't know what. A low, yet audible, noise is heard a purring of some sort. The head-splitting sound grows at a constant rate. You finally realise what the sound is... a huntsman spider. But this creature of immense size could not possibly be it, this is something much more sinister...

## Glen Bracken (13)
St Richard's Catholic College, Bexhill-On-Sea

# REVENANT

One day, you go to an abandoned church to investigate a murder.

As you walk down the aisle towards the altar, black crows fly away. The church is overgrown and eerie. You find a mutilated, bloody body on the floor. Suddenly, you turn around as the candles light up on their own. Then you see a creature wearing a pale goat skull. It's quite tall. It starts to walk towards you and picks you up by the neck.

"What the hell are you?"

It replies, "Death..."

You stop hearing and your vision goes blurry until everything goes black...

## Harry Rouse (13)
St Richard's Catholic College, Bexhill-On-Sea

# YOU CAN HIDE FROM THE DEVIL, BUT HE'LL ALWAYS FIND YOU

I entered hesitantly onto the screeching floorboards into the gloomy cellar... I clutched the lantern in my hand whilst it illuminated the darkness. I peered in front of me. I felt my cheeks burn. My mouth fell open, my head began to spin. Suddenly, I heard its sharp, careless footsteps prowling behind me. I could smell its fumes of rotting flesh and its shallow breathing as it dragged its aroma through my nose and mouth, causing me to gag in agony. My stomach twisted terribly as its savagely contorted and mangled hands gripped my waist. The Devil had been unleashed!

## Besiana Martinaj (14)
St Richard's Catholic College, Bexhill-On-Sea

# THE LEGEND OF THE FIVE SPIRITS

The five walked up to the house and opened the door, peering inside.

They went up the stairs, as quick but as quiet as possible. All of a sudden, they heard whispering, first quiet, but then loud enough to hear.

"Take the knife from the bathroom..."

"Get out of here before it happens!"

"Humans... kill them..."

They all froze in their tracks. They turned around and ran down the stairs two at a time. They all tripped over. Three of them broke their necks. Two of them died. No one knows what happened next...

**Renisse Gregorio (13)**
St Richard's Catholic College, Bexhill-On-Sea

# SCARED. ALONE. TERRIFIED

Another night, just like any other. The sounds of screaming foxes from the woods and of music from parties next door. A nice, peaceful, night.

The comfort of my bedsheets. The chaotic sound of a police chase outside.

A calm, peaceful, night.

I drifted off. Glass shattered, I heard footsteps. I didn't move. I was scared. What was happening? My mind was blank, yet I had thoughts rushing through my head. It was unbearable.

Why were they here? Who was here? What did they want? I felt trapped in my own body. I was scared. Alone. Terrified.

## Finley Hide (13)
St Richard's Catholic College, Bexhill-On-Sea

# ATTACHMENT

I had not existed.

I stumbled across hospital corridors among the sick and dying, those gasping for salvation and saving from their fates.

Such familiar emotions, emotions that I would only know until I met you among the strangled shrieks and blood-splattered sheets. Fear was the only thing I knew until I met you. When calloused hands grip at you, clutching at you like vultures to a corpse. Our eyes burst with tears, our skin growing cold and clammy. I burn, I know only flame. My brain is full of screaming voices and I know that this is forever.

**Ivy Weeks-Pearson (13)**
St Richard's Catholic College, Bexhill-On-Sea

# THE FOREST

I'd been separated from the group, stranded, all alone. The wind wasn't holding back. I was scared I'd never find my way out of the woods. I just wanted to stay home by the warm fire, but I was dragged out.

The trees were like towers. All I could see was a tainted dark blue. There was a silhouette coming closer. It was running towards me.

"Help!" I shouted, begging him to help me home.

He had an object in his hand and a weak flashlight. He was getting closer and I knew one thing... he wasn't here to save me.

## Zoe Pisani-Cleland (15)
St Richard's Catholic College, Bexhill-On-Sea

# TRIBAN TOWER

Triban Tower was gone. Forever. Now, you may wonder why it was called that. Thirty years ago, there was a young boy who lived there. He was called Triban because he had three lives.

You may be thinking, wow three lives! But no. It was the complete opposite. You see, he only had three lives which meant he had three chances to take over the world.

He failed the first two times but the third time, he succeeded. He took over the world. That's why the tower was called Triban Tower. But, someone else wanted to takeover the world too...

## Carla Herring (12)
St Richard's Catholic College, Bexhill-On-Sea

# THE WINDOW CREATURE

It began on a cold, dark night. Something stalked the roads, like an animal on the prowl. Blood dripped from its fangs and a manic laugh echoed.
In his house, Jay was watching Game of Thrones on his laptop. He had no idea of the danger that lurked outside. The creature slowly dragged its claws through the door and the handles unlocked. Jay was too busy to notice as the windows slowly opened. Suddenly, the room went cold. Jay stopped what he was doing and turned to the window. His heart stopped...

## Rory Eade (16)
St Richard's Catholic College, Bexhill-On-Sea

# HELP ME

I couldn't move. I could barely breathe. I felt a cold wrinkly hand wrap itself around my arm. I was suddenly on the floor. There was a jet-black door in front of me. It was open. I heard a scream and decided to investigate. That was a mistake.

I walked along the corridor. I smelt the awful scent of eggs. My shoes were wet... wet with blood. I wanted to get out of there. I got to the entrance and it was locked! I panicked. I heard footsteps behind me. I was trapped...

**Jessica Cart (11)**
St Richard's Catholic College, Bexhill-On-Sea

# PANDEMIC

Walking along the dirty street, the flickering streetlights above emit rotten orange hues, weaving up the darkened alleyway ahead. You begin to notice that small feeling inside you, making your stomach crawl. You begin to regret volunteering for that investigation...

After a while of eerie silence, disturbed only by the lonesome clicking of black leather shoes, you look before you, dread crawls up your throat. You catch a glimpse of a swinging body through the ajar door.

"Not here as well?!"

Panic-stricken, you click your radio.

"Sergeant! Quarantine on Ivy Town ASAP. It's spread here too!"

## Seth Tomes (13)

Staffordshire University Academy, Hednesford

# DON'T TURN AROUND

Jack was there beside me. It was his idea to come.
He stepped inside, the floorboards made a loud creak.
"What was that?" he whispered.
We walked in further. *Bang!* The front door slammed behind us. No one was there.
"Phew!"
We entered the living room and a glass shattered in the kitchen. Ignoring it, we looked at the graffiti.
"Others explored here before," Jack said.
There was something about this graffiti that wasn't right. It said: 'Get out!' and 'Don't turn around!' I felt something touch my neck, ice-cold and damp!
Reluctantly, we turned around...

## Dominic Jones (12)
Staffordshire University Academy, Hednesford

# HOW MANY TIMES!

"Jake, what are you doing?" Steven said.
"How many times do I have to tell you? It will get you nowhere not listening to me!"
"Steven, just let the process go, mate. What's the worst that can happen?" Jake prompted.
The two boys continued to stroll down the cracked up path, where trees had been broken and plants were overgrown.
"Look!" shouted Steven. "How did you not see that huge manly shadow?"
At this point, Steven was frightened. They walked a bit more. The boys started to regret doing this. Then Jake made Steven...

## Sam Stanton (14)
Staffordshire University Academy, Hednesford

# THE LAST (HAUNTED) HOUSE ON THE LEFT!

We walked through a creepy forest with abandoned houses.
I said, "Everyone ready? Are you sure?"
A speaker on the wall said, "Come through to the house, kiddies."
We walked through and saw a house. It had dark green trees covering it so you couldn't see it at all. I walked past it first and nothing happened. Then my friends walked past and the lights inside flickered on and off.
"Run!" Alex shouted as loud as he could.
I ran a different way and never saw my friends again.
What should I do? Stay or go and find them?

## Mason Whittingham (13)
Staffordshire University Academy, Hednesford

# GHOST STORIES

"Oh, come on, it will be fun!" she stated, making her way to the woods.

"Yes, because going into the woods when we have heard the stories is so much fun!" Tom answered back, trembling.

"Those stories probably aren't even real," Alyssa replied.

The two friends went into the woods in the dead of night, what wasn't fun about that? Except for one thing... the beast that lived among them.

"Hurry up, Tom!" Alyssa shouted, waking the beast.

"I'm coming. Where even are you?" he whispered.

But Alyssa had disappeared...

## Molly Duffy (13)
Staffordshire University Academy, Hednesford

# CLOSE YOUR EYES

Right.
Cotton buds filled their brain, soaking up each and every thought. It threw their pace off balance.
Left.
A feeling snuck up the back of their neck, creeping along their hair. Falling around it, entangling into knots. The type you couldn't untangle. A sixth sense.
Right.
So close, yet so incredibly far. The feeling heightened as if a hand was grasping onto the back of their neck. Fingernails so harsh, digging in, drawing blood. It stung. Fear welled up in their throat. Growing and growing. It hurt so bad.
A voice echoed, yet no one had spoken...

## Izzy Brown-Jones (13)
Staffordshire University Academy, Hednesford

# IN THE FOREST

The broken mud path led to the old trees. Glimmering off the trees, the moonlight was slowly covered by grey fluff. It left the deep forest filled with darkness. Slowly walking, I could hear a spine-chilling noise. *Snap!* I thought the forest was empty. Was I not alone?

Fear filled the air and I knew it wasn't just me who lurked in the darkness. Paranoia hit me, it felt like there were noises everywhere. It didn't feel safe
wherever I went... A shadow! It looked like it was getting closer to me. Something grabbed me, I knew it was over...

## Mia Collins-Hodgetts (12)
Staffordshire University Academy, Hednesford

# KEEP OUT

The moonlight cast its glow onto the pale white manor, and the 'Keep out' sign urging me to turn back.

I pushed the rusty gate open. There was a strange silence about the place, creepy. I went in and the door quickly slammed shut behind me. *Click! Huh?* I thought to myself as I climbed up the stairs.

There was one room at the end of the corridor. As I slowly crept forwards, it slowly got warmer.

I opened the door. In the room was a pale, charred boy. "Help... me," he said.

Suddenly, I could smell smoke...

## Seth Gray (13)
Staffordshire University Academy, Hednesford

# THE FEELING

You stride through the door. There is a staircase. The creak of the floorboards sends chills down your spine.
You slowly walk up the stairs with caution. You think you hear a voice. It might be your imagination. You don't want to stay still. You feel like you may be attacked.
You move to another room. You're in a bedroom. The atmosphere is freezing. *Ding-dong! Ding-dong!* You hear the clocks weeping the call to the world. Maybe someone else is here. Maybe it's all hallucinations and none of it is real. Then you feel it...

## Alex Corns (12)
Staffordshire University Academy, Hednesford

# HOW DID I GET HERE?

On a pitch-black chilling night. I found myself stranded and petrified in a misty wood. I had no way of contacting the outside world and I need somewhere to stay for the night. My spine chilled as I took each step further. I heard blood-curdling screams in the distance. Suddenly, I saw the eerie shadow of a cottage. My only choice was to investigate. The cottage was covered in what looked like veins.

I cautiously opened the large creaking door and stepped in. My panic levels were high as the door slammed behind me. I had walked into hell...

**Jack Robinson (13)**
Staffordshire University Academy, Hednesford

# HE'S BACK

I woke up to a humming noise followed by laughter. I looked around my room frantically, trying to see where it was coming from. But as soon as I met with those eyes, those eyes I wished to forget forever, I knew I was in trouble. Suddenly, all I could hear was the rapid thumping of my heartbeat in my ears.

"Why are you here?" I asked, mentally cursing myself for stuttering.

The words that came out of his mouth sent a chill down my spine.

"I have some unfinished business," he said with a sickening smirk.

## Lilly Gooch (13)
Staffordshire University Academy, Hednesford

# SHADOWS OF THE NIGHT

I walked past the towering trees, sticks and leaves crunching beneath my feet. I looked through the fog of the night sky and saw it in the distance. My walking suddenly turned into a sprint. I looked up, amazed at the overgrown house I saw when I was younger.

Lightning struck, illuminating the wall beside me. I jumped. A shadow suddenly ran across the wall. I knew I wasn't alone. I took one last look at the haunted manor and ran until I suddenly blacked out.

I woke up but I didn't realize that the shadow was in my room...

## Jack Dunne (13)
Staffordshire University Academy, Hednesford

# A DATE WITH DEATH

Vines crept down the cragged walls as I begrudgingly entered. Why would they want to meet here? Why couldn't we go somewhere else for the date instead? I would've knocked on the vast, overshadowing door; if there was one. I walked in, half expecting nobody, half expecting a hot date to be waiting for me. Something was waiting, but not that. A looming figure wandered aimlessly in my direction. Turning to run, I froze in fear as it closed in. This was no typical date. This was a date... but a date with death.

## Danielle Morning (13)
Staffordshire University Academy, Hednesford

# HER FACE...

"Help..."
Her body dropped to the floor. I was speechless. *Why her?* I thought, still not able to take my eyes off the lifeless body. Then I heard it. He was here. I had to run. Quickly. I ran and ran. He caught up with me. How could I get out? I didn't want to be here. Help!
Did he just walk past me? I was right out in the open. Without thinking, I headed over to the body. She was still dead. I turned her over, looking at her face. Wait. I froze again. It was me. I'm... dead?

## Eva Hopkins (13)
Staffordshire University Academy, Hednesford

# IS IT A SPIRIT OR AM I JUST TERRIFIED?

Walking through the eerie house, floorboards creaked as I passed. The atmosphere around me felt as though there was a spirit around me. I looked at my surroundings. As I looked to my left, a mirror that I spotted while I was looking to my right, had dropped and smashed. *It could be the wind*, I thought, though the mirror was secure on the wall.
As I was already creeped out, I quickened my pace. Then the door that I had walked through slammed. I tried to move. But I couldn't. I felt pinned down.

**Chloe Harrison (13)**
Staffordshire University Academy, Hednesford

# DON'T MOVE

It was a cold windy night when I was out with my friend, Bailey. Suddenly, we heard the spine-chilling sound of a girl crying.

"What on earth was that noise?" Bailey asked.

"Bailey, I saw about this on the news," I told Bailey.

"What?" Bailey asked.

"It said if you hear a girl crying, or you see her call the police straight away," I explained.

"Harvey, don't move..." said Bailey.

There was someone behind me. Was it the crying girl?

**Harvey Duke (12)**
Staffordshire University Academy, Hednesford

# LOST

I'd been wandering for about three hours when I found an abandoned castle. I decided to take a look inside. It was crumbling with debris on the floor. If I had to guess, it had probably been left for about twenty years. That was older than me! I kept looking around, hoping I would find some lost treasure. I guess not though.

I had been exploring for about an hour and it had gotten quite dark outside. I should probably head back, but which way was it?

Was I... was I lost?

## Chloe Julian (13)
Staffordshire University Academy, Hednesford

# THE GRAVEYARD

As I entered the isolated woods, I saw an abandoned graveyard. Not one grave had been left untouched. Caskets were everywhere. Someone had dug up the graves...
In the far distance, a flickering candle danced in the howling wind. A shady figure walked with a shovel. He wore a dark mask and left a damp paper note. He had created a crime scene to commit an even bigger one.
I turned around. The tall dark figure was towering over me with the shovel...

## Nathan Collins (14)
Staffordshire University Academy, Hednesford

# THE BROKEN BOY

The Broken Boy was a myth, spread throughout the small town about a boy who loved but was never loved. The little boy would come out to play, stealing the hearts of lovers and the souls of the loved.

It was the dead of night with no one around and no one awake. There was no place to hide because hell was on the loose. Don't turn your back, don't face the moon and definitely don't love unless you want to play the game of The Broken Boy...

## Shannon Tomkinson (13)
Staffordshire University Academy, Hednesford

# TRICK OR TREAT?

One Halloween night, a fifteen-year-old girl called Mary was walking through a forest with her friends.
After a while, they heard a rustling in the bushes. At first, they thought it was the wind. The rustling continued and they started to see black figures running across the paths. She asked her friends to stop walking. There was no response... they were already dead.
She tried to ask if someone was there. The figure had been behind her the whole time!

## Finlay Hull (12)
Staffordshire University Academy, Hednesford

# DISAPPEAR

"Josh, stop!" shouted Jeff while shaking with fear.

"No, I've already gone this far, I might as well go all the way," Josh shouted back while walking towards the old church by the cliff.

Jeff was trembling uncontrollably while he shouted to Josh, "No! People have gone there and never come back. That's why it's taped off!"

Just as he said that there was a scream...

Josh had disappeared...

## Charlie Brockhurst (14)

Staffordshire University Academy, Hednesford

# I BECAME IT, AND IT BECAME ME

I entered the sinister place where I became it and it became me. I felt its poison consume my soul. It felt like medicine. I was glad of the company and no longer felt the relentless emptiness within myself.

Silence lingered in the stagnant air. Suddenly, it was rippled by an echoing voice...

"Death becomes you, beautiful girl, and you become death..."

I entered the sinister place where I became it and it became me, though I never escaped. My soul blackened by poison, and my beauty lost in the darkness.

For death is not company, it is eternal loneliness.

**Poppy Lacey (17)**
Suffolk One, Pinewood

# JEALOUSY

The girl had glass-like dark blue eyes that stared deep into Chloe's. Her hair was like wire and brushed into a perfect bob. Her face was ghosted like the child was possessed and had been there for 100 years, there when this house was made a century ago, in 1820.

Chloe felt daunted and distanced.

Annie looked, sounded and played like a doll.

"Come play with me!" Annie cried. "Why won't you play with me?"

The next day was Tuesday, Chloe played with another girl.

Annie saw and Chloe was never seen again.

Sometimes you can still hear crying. Sobbing.

## Alice Dibb (13)
Swanmore College, Swanmore

# UNSEEN

At the time of the event, the street went dark; the music stopped. Then sirens went off. All parents rushed inside with their children, keeping them all hidden, locking their doors. Later that night, a little girl called Rose looked outside her bedroom window and glanced out at the street but there wasn't anything or anyone there. As she looked away from the window, something whispered, "Come closer, come closer...

Ten seconds later, the power went out. It was pitch-black. The voice, Anzel, dragged Rose through the wall. She became one of the Unseen!

**Lillie Vivian (14)**
Swanmore College, Swanmore

# ALONE AND FORGOTTEN

Like an eternally pained eye, my door screamed open in one final protest. Ancient wood and brittle nails adhering together to my tainted walls. Hidden under my refuge of scraggly blankets and weakened wooden frame, I could hear them. You know, the drummers' steady beat. The Devil's heart throb.

Footsteps marched to guide me off my mortal coil and drip evil like sickening paint. As though it were magnified, lead-black ink slunk towards me. Gagging my screams and blinding my tearing orbs. I could hear them. You know, the Angels of Death, my only companions.

## Chloe Harvey
Swanmore College, Swanmore

# THE CUDDLY STABBER

Ali's old, blue car pulled up into Thornwell Drive, gravel crunched and crackled as it went. The young graduate opened her car door and looked up at the Victorian house. She opened the creaking door. She saw a doll. She picked it up and read an old, torn label: 'Rosebud'.
Ali shrugged and placed it on the side. She continued through the house. The doll wobbled and let out a small cackle. It very clumsily stood up, wandered to the kitchen and picked up a worn knife, stained with brown blood. It let out an even louder cackle...

## Archie C (12)
Swanmore College, Swanmore

# THE MONSTER

He gasped, begging for air as his bloodshot eyes widened. His arms shook violently and his face was as white as snow. The sudden realisation that this unwanted reality he had entered, was nothing but a dream, hit him like a bullet in the head.

Relieved, yet still recovering from shock, he started to clamber out of his creaky bed. The visions flashed before him of the monster's spiked ears, mustard eyes and razor-sharp pointed teeth.

He sat still, shaking on the bed until he felt a hand. No! A claw clutch his frail ankle...

## Sophie Smith (12)
Swanmore College, Swanmore

# CREEPY ECLIPSE...

You walk through the cracked wooden door. You look down the musty, shadowy hallway. You breathe in the invisible, polluted, dusty air. You come to face a mystical creepy creature. It's tall and you can't make out its shape. You look down trembling. What is it?
You hear its shallow breathing and its thumping heart echo through the tall, mystical, haunted house. You don't understand what it wants, or what it is, or what it's going to do. All you hope is that it hasn't seen you and it won't kill you... What it really was, was hope...

**Elisa Gjoka (13)**
Sydney Russell School, Dagenham

# CURIOSITY

My curiosity had once again got the better of me. I had some sort of desperate need to look. I was fully certain all my cravings would melt away if I could just have a single peep. This once, I would give in to the hunger. Satisfy my human desire. I would look just once. My body was held prisoner to my mind.

Before I knew it, my eye was level with the keyhole.

To this day, I had no clue of what I had seen. All that mattered to me was my carnal desire to feed.

**Ruth Ogbuokiri (13)**
Sydney Russell School, Dagenham

# THE RAMPAGE DOLL

Once, there was a terrifying doll named Annabelle. She was about three foot tall with an extraordinarily large axe. She ran about the town chasing every man. She turned all of the men in town into face painted clowns with horrible sharp teeth. She possessed all the women. She made the possessed women fight the ugly clowns.

All the children chased Annabelle with their kitchen knives and caught her. One kid tied her up in a dark tunnel, telling her to turn all their families back.

She said, "No!"

The kids killed her. Then everything went back to normal.

**Kieron Batey (14)**
The Beacon Centre, South Shields

# CRAZY MAN

On July 12th, on a dark street in Gateshead, a deranged man sat on a wall waving a knife around. Suddenly, he jumped down and started to run around the streets screaming like a mad man.

All of a sudden, he stopped. His eye was drawn to a young lady walking all alone.

He went behind her and started following her down the road. She didn't notice him until she was in her house. She looked out of the window to see him looking back at her. Smiling. Waving the knife in front of him...

## Faith Brown (13)
The Beacon Centre, South Shields

# THE MAN WHO KNEW ME

I had just finished a long day of school, it was about
3.30pm. I was waiting for the bus. Behind me was an old
man. I thought he was following me. I got on the bus, when
it arrived; he got on too.

It was now 4.30pm and pitch-black. He got off the bus when
I got off. It was still a five-minute walk through the wood.
Behind me, I heard the twigs snapping. I turned around. He
was there with a machete. I didn't know what to do. Did he
know where I lived...?

## Callum Fontaine (12)

The Beacon Centre, South Shields

# THE BEGINNING, MIDDLE, AND END

In a society where the population was held to a bare minimum, government parties declared only one child per household. The Morettis' never faced a problem with this, until the year 2126.

If leaders discovered a family having more than one, murder was obligated. Jane was an only child, until May 7th 2126. The unforgettable news came to her when she was sitting in her mother's chair. She could never forget the words, "Jane, we need to leave."

It went dark.

"Come back, Jane!" he screamed.

His anger poured out, as the rain intensified.

## Paige Whittaker (15)
The Gateway Academy, Tilbury

# RED MIST

They asked me what I remembered.

I was frozen in time. A hazy mist unfurled around the tips of skeletal trees which looked faint to me. The setting was drenched in darkness. The inky darkness was all I could see until I espied a glint of light that ricocheted off metallic dark feathers and intense red eyes like congealed blood. The darkness around me, fragile like glass, was shattered by its call. Followed by a scream.

I ran towards the sound. It was then I saw the blood, the redness flowing like a stream.

"That's all I remember..." I said.

## Gia Bhalla (12)
The Henrietta Barnett School, Hampstead Garden Suburb

# I HAVE TO SAVE HIM

I heard it. *Creak!* She was here. This was it... where my life would end. I could think of no better reason to die than protecting him.

She entered, a mischievous glint in her eyes. Panic. She smiled.

"I killed him! Just seconds ago!"

Nooo!

"Kathrine! You gave me your word!"

The last thing I saw was my alarm clock flashing 1.02am before she dug her piercing nails into my flesh, paralyzing my body...

I sat bolt upright, relieved it was just a dream. Then I saw the clock bearing 1.00am.

Oh no! Landon. I have to save him...

## Hannah Boolaky (12)
The Henrietta Barnett School, Hampstead Garden Suburb

# THAT NIGHT

It was just past midnight. I clambered into bed after an exhausting day at work. I was closing my eyes when I heard a creak. I shot up and looked around wildly but there was nothing there.

"It's the wind," I reassured myself and settled back down. Then I heard it again. It sounded closer this time. My heart pounded in my chest. *Creak!* My breath came out in short, panicked gasps as the cupboard opened. A taloned foot stepped out and large, bulbous eyes stared at me. Its mouth was stretched into a perfect Cheshire cat grin. I screamed.

## Aishwarya Kozhikkottu Mundakkaparambil (13)
The Henrietta Barnett School, Hampstead Garden Suburb

# CAN YOU BREAK A BROKEN HEART?

Old Bert had always lived in the wooden hut on the top of the hill if you were to ask at the closest village. It was as if he had sprung to life as he was now, wizened, old, alone, paralysed. Broken.

No one remembered where he'd come from, the alien from the planet none other than pain.

Inside the hut, Bert's gaunt gaze, his sunken eyes, were fixed on the blade his own shaking arm was directing to his chest. He wondered, or maybe pleaded, for the yearned-for, long-awaited emptiness.

Can you break a broken heart?

## Sofia Kountouri (12)
The Henrietta Barnett School, Hampstead Garden Suburb

# NEWS FLASH

Gloom gathered as the lightning laughed. The TV was turned on in a near deafening silence so Michael's parents wouldn't wake from their slumber. Mike had seen everything; the mason of the living room lay in ornate fashion as the cosy home battled against the daunting thunder. The terrier that lay on Michael's lap lay as still as a statue...

Then a breaking news flash halted the screen.

"A family of four have been classified missing, vanishing completely from their home, no trace was left apart from an open backdoor..."

Michael heard the unmistakable sound of a window being opened...

## Calin Neagu. (12)

The Magna Carta School, Staines-Upon-Thames

# TRAPPED!

The wind howled out in pain, lightning flashed across the sky whilst the windows rattled, opening, and shutting, screaming for help. This time, it was real pain. The area craved for anything that it could get, anything that it could trap in its grasp. Why? You may ask. Why are people trapped in natural things around a house?
The house in question was haunted and the answer was, because of the man who lived there. The man in question was old, with short, grey hair and sunken, lifeless eyes. Sunken lifeless eyes that were being controlled by something. Something powerful...

## Joshua Makepeace (12)
The Magna Carta School, Staines-Upon-Thames

# THE CURSE OF THE LOST PYRAMID

Kase was hot, sweaty and tired. He'd been looking for the 'cursed' pyramid for years now, determined to find it. A worker came in.

"Sir," he panted, "We think we found something."

Kase sat up so fast he hit his head. He didn't care.

The pyramid was dark and dismal, with too many traps. He'd already lost a squad to a pit of cobras. They turned a corner. There it was, the sarcophagus of the Pharoah Ahmentoped. He opened it and... nothing. The last thing Kase remembered was looking down, watching himself dust away. Forever.

## James Burdett (12)

The Magna Carta School, Staines-Upon-Thames

# DISCONNECTED FROM REALITY

I opened my eyes. I couldn't recognize where I was, everything around me was white. I looked at my hands and they were a little off centre. They were ghost-like, and my movement was slow. I became terrified. As I screamed, I couldn't hear myself.

Slowly, I saw other shapes moving past me. My hearing gradually came back and the voices around me became louder and louder.

They were saying, "You can't escape..."

Thoughts of home became very strong in my mind. I remembered the fight I had with my Mum. I missed her. It was over for me...

## Iona Ogilvie (12)
The Magna Carta School, Staines-Upon-Thames

# MURDER'S DOOR

Placing the cigar on the ashtray, smoke crushed on the scruffy surface. Blood trickled down my face and nerves shocked my spine. The death, the shame, did not faze me. Graveyards filled whilst I sat in my car, watching from afar, laughing at the weeping of families losses.
The wine-red blood spilt everywhere. I stepped out, leaving a note to tell the world these eighteen deaths were caused by one man, that man was me. The note read: 'Sins have been committed and I'm glad I did it'. Getting back in the car, innocent lives would soon be taken away...

**Ollie Bailey**
The Magna Carta School, Staines-Upon-Thames

# THE HOUSE THAT HAUNTED

Mika and her little sister, Clara, pulled up at the crooked cottage in their little red Corsa. It had been several days since their late mother passed and now Gran was looking after them.

Whilst unpacking the boot, Mika spotted a small figure standing in the attic window. She was confused. Gran was much taller than that. The door creaked as they opened it. There was no Gran. Suddenly, the door slammed shut and the small figure appeared at the top of the staircase.

"Why?" Clara screamed, they both did. The lights went out and that was that... Gone!

## Megan Young (12)
The Magna Carta School, Staines-Upon-Thames

# DAD!

I slammed the door. My throat was sore from yelling. How could they be so cruel? I was going to the only one who cared, Dad.
I raced through the streets, on and on, down the winding roads. Finally, I reached the village church.
The crooked gate to the graveyard creaked open. Chills ran down my spine something was different tonight...
The sky was a dark blue, darker than normal. The wind had vanished. Everything was quiet. I looked for the curved stone in the distance, my dad. But there in its place stood a hooded figure with gleaming eyes...

## Maeve Parkin (12)
The Magna Carta School, Staines-Upon-Thames

# THE PHOTOGRAPH

Ella slowly opened the antique, elegantly engraved box that was wrapped in a thick layer of dust like a blanket. Opening the box, her attention was drawn to a photograph. It looked fragile and faded, so much so that it took all of her ability to make out the image.

A smile gradually appeared on her face as she recognised her parents happily sat together in a field of dandelions and daisies. She turned over the photo. Her eyes widened when she saw the date. It said: 'Lilian and Edward, 1826'. This made her parents over one hundred years old...

## Milly Clark (12)
The Magna Carta School, Staines-Upon-Thames

# A FLY IN A SPIDER'S WEB

The room was dark. The lights had gone out. I was all alone. No roommate to hang out with, no friend to talk to over the phone. It was just me and the suspiciously empty apartment building. Not a single footstep of the neighbours walking nor the sound of doors opening or closing. Just me and the locked entrance doors of the building. No way to get in or out. Completely trapped like a fly in a spiderweb. It was completely silent.

Suddenly, there were loud, thumping footsteps running towards me, getting louder. It sounded like the spider had awoken.

## Nadia Swierczynska (12)

The Magna Carta School, Staines-Upon-Thames

# THE GIRL THAT WAS REBORN

Mia and Luca were a very good-looking couple. Mia gave birth to a girl, but she looked nothing like her parents.
One day, the couple took her to their favourite park on the edge of a cliff. They walked closer to the edge and threw her off.
Years later, Mia gave birth to another girl and named her Lucy. Once Lucy turned four, the couple took her to their favourite park. As soon as they stepped in, Lucy made a huge scene.
"No Mummy! Please don't throw me off again. I came back pretty for you! Don't you love me?"

## Ilke Savas (12)
The Magna Carta School, Staines-Upon-Thames

# THE WISH

Once, there was a little boy. He wanted to go to the stream. He went to see his friends but no one answered. He remembered that he'd found a wishing well in the woods. He went there and wished for more friends.

Suddenly, two people said, "Hello, can we be your friends?" He replied, "Yes!"

But then things got weird. People started dying. His friends started laughing about it.

The boy went back to the wishing well and wished for everything to go back to normal but his friends killed him...

## Seth Fisher (11)
The Magna Carta School, Staines-Upon-Thames

# THE GHOST OF THE ESTATE

You walk into the creaking, dusty, ancient manor estate, hoping to find aged artefacts. As you wipe away the cobwebs, twisting over your dry, bruised skin, you hear a high-pitched screech from a young girl. It comes to your ear, sending shivers and goosebumps down your body. The hair on your skin shoots up.

You decide to go towards the screech to help the young girl. You get to the room and open the door... It crackles and the handle falls off. You enter the room cautiously. Then out of nowhere, a ghost enters your withered soul.

## Ethan Woods (12)
The Magna Carta School, Staines-Upon-Thames

# APOCALYPSE

I was sitting on the bus talking with my friend on the way to school. Suddenly, a dark luminous green portal opened up. People started screaming, running from zombies and monsters. I smashed open the window in the bus and ran to my treehouse. I wasn't paying attention to where I was going and ran straight into a zombie. Luckily, I escaped!
I was in the treehouse, figuring out how to save the world when I heard my stomach rumbling. I decided to go to the shop.
On the way, I bumped into a zombie. I was being chased...

**Adam Hiley (12)**
The Magna Carta School, Staines-Upon-Thames

# THE ORPHANAGE

Dear Diary,

I'm fortunate and delighted to have a caring family full of forsaken children and a Mama.

Not knowing cold or hollow, we live healthily and satisfied about what we have. We exist without knowing the world outside; the barriers around the field shut the freedom to fly; the gate Mama told us not to go there. Never ever. The untold truth behind the gates walked a path of blackness, gore and full of beasts, flooding. Waiting to slaughter us. My heart felt like a white Vida flower but blooming red.

## Dhiyana Padmanabhan (12)

The Magna Carta School, Staines-Upon-Thames

# PATIENT

You know that feeling we all get when we're alone? That feeling that somebody's watching? Scary right?
I was waiting in a forest one night for my Scout group to come back. I waited for hours. Patient.
It wasn't until I heard a howl and a gush of wind brush my damp, decaying tent that I got worried they weren't coming back. I felt a gush of wind brush past my face and a growl. I could tell someone was there. Was it my Scout group playing a trick on me? Or was it something else...?

## Charlie Cotsworth (12)
The Magna Carta School, Staines-Upon-Thames

# HER...

I lost everything I had and loved because of her. It took five years to prove my innocence and for people to learn to trust me again.

Ana blamed me for killing a group of teenagers and my life ready to be buried... but now it was time for hers to be.

It was barely enough for her to be behind bars so I had to take a different direction and finish this feud now. I had to kill her, eliminate her.

When the warm blood trembled between my fingers, I knew I liked it maybe a little too much.

## Jemimah Ahmed (13)
The Magna Carta School, Staines-Upon-Thames

# THE DARK

I was always scared of the dark. Today was the day I thought it wouldn't be such a good day to go out when it was pitch-black.
I was in the forest. Gradually walking, I felt an eerie atmosphere. I felt a scratch on my arm. That was when I knew I was not alone.
I looked to my left and right. I saw nothing in the big tall trees. I looked behind me. I was shocked. There was a black massive figure. It was getting closer and closer. I ran faster and faster. I screamed. It was the end...

## Tanya Kawenya (12)
The Magna Carta School, Staines-Upon-Thames

# COGS

I didn't know who I was, but I knew I was trapped. The floor, walls and roof were made of cogs. The wall opened. A robot rolled through, with a spinning saw blade in hand. I ran around it and hit it.

The wall opened up. I went through as it closed behind me. I came to a large control room, surrounded by more cogs. I knew what I had to do. I slammed the buttons to shut down the robots, but cut my arm, revealing cogs underneath. I was a robot! The system shut down and so did I.

## Luke Balaam (12)
The Magna Carta School, Staines-Upon-Thames

# WHAT IF?

There I was, stranded in the middle of the forbidden forest, surrounded by a life of lies.

I had lost my dog, my way and my mind. I had no other option than to run, but where to go? What path to take? Who to tell? What would I do? Who would even want to help me? I know I wouldn't.

Suddenly, I froze in fear. The ghostly man, he could be out there, watching, waiting, listening. What if he followed me? What if he stole my dog or what if he was the reason I was going insane?

## Summer Digby (11)

The Magna Carta School, Staines-Upon-Thames

# THE MAN UNDER THE MASK!

It was a gloomy night. No one knew where they had gone or where they were. The cold air brushed past my hair as it flowed in the wind. I rapidly started to walk as I heard footsteps creeping behind me. I was terrified.
All of a sudden, I felt like I was being dragged backwards. My heart felt like it had skipped a beat. I felt a cold shiver run down my spine. I tried to look at their face but I could see nothing. That was all I remembered. All I saw was a man under a mask.

## Chloe Wells
The Magna Carta School, Staines-Upon-Thames

# THE DARK FIGURE

I watched from my window. A figure appeared from the darkness. It was dressed all in black with a ghostly shadow beneath. Its eyes were bloodshot and deep red. The figure stood, staring at my house from the darkness.

I fled upstairs when it came running, locking the door behind me. I heard footsteps from below. Suddenly, there was a loud banging on the door. It was forced open. Slowly, the creature entered, smiling. It held a knife in one hand...

**Dylan Rodriguez (12)**
The Magna Carta School, Staines-Upon-Thames

# THE GHOSTS OF CARISBROOKE

I stumbled to the castle and heard the heavy wind whistling. I made my way up the steps, peering over the crumbling castle wall to see the bowling green in the far distance. As I dragged my hands along the brick wall, I found King Charles' old sleeping chambers.

"I can't believe I've discovered this!" I muttered softly under my breath.

I made my way to the bowling green. I felt a lump in my throat. I felt something hit the back of my shoe. I look behind me to see a bowling ball. In a flash, it was gone...

## Zoe Thorne (15)
The Quay School, Parkstone

# THE BLOODY BUILDING

The door was wide open. The house was stood tall like a bodyguard. I slowly walked inside.

It was dark and there was a horrid, putrid odour wafting through the building. I took a few more steps, wandering in and out of the different rooms. I felt eyes on me like I was being watched.

Out of the corner of my eye, I saw something strange. I went into the kitchen. There was blood everywhere. It was splattered across the walls. I felt like I couldn't breathe. I rapidly turned around. A tall figure was standing in the doorway...

**Amy Heyward-Allen (16)**
The Quay School, Parkstone

# THALASSOPHOBIA

I woke to find myself floating in the middle of a vast ocean alone on my rubber ring, freezing cold and soaking wet. Last thing I could remember was being on the beach with my friends. It was pitch-black, apart from comets and meteors hurtling through the sky.

I could see things in the water. Were they reflections of the meteor shower or were they creatures stirred up by it? I heard a thunderous sound and looked down to see enormous blood-red eyes peering at me through the darkness. Teeth were coming up towards me...

## Jacob Thompson (15)
The Quay School, Parkstone

# A NIGHT TO REMEMBER

The fog crept in. It was a dark stormy night. The town was empty. I could feel drops of rain running down my back. I shivered. I ran as fast as I could to find shelter. I found an old abandoned mansion.

The door opened. I shouldn't have, but I was drawn in. I heard strange noises but there was no one in sight. I felt something go past me but there was nothing there. As I looked in the window, a mysterious black shadow appeared. I heard the doors slam and lock. I felt teeth in my neck...

## Alfie Lambert (15)
The Quay School, Parkstone

# THE MYSTERIOUS GRAVEYARD

One evening inside the snug cottage, a girl called Lucy was sitting in her living room waiting to go to the peculiar graveyard that sat lonely behind her house.

As she grabbed her coat and walked outside, she felt an ice-cold chill. She approached the graveyard and heard an ear-splitting scream. All of a sudden, she saw a creature. It had blood-red eyes and a hairy back with bleeding spikes. Once she saw the creature, she shrieked and sprinted home, petrified by what she saw.

After that day, she never left her house again...

## Sophie Pasfield (12)
The Stanway School, Stanway

# THE TRAIN

The wind rushed through my hair as the train barrelled through the station. It screeched to a halt and I stepped on. Another day, another three train rides to school. I wish I'd known what was going to happen when I leapt on the train...

It was halfway through the first journey when the train began screaming as the brakes clung to the rails. I was jolted off my seat and flung to the floor. Then the lights went off. Darkness. The silence hung in the air as a scream cut through it like a knife. The door swung open...

**Finlay Panther**
The Stanway School, Stanway

# THE BLOOD MOON PARTY!

It happened on a day just like this, in a room just like this. Four friends were having a blood moon party.

"Gimme what I'm owed, gimme what I'm owed," a voice hissed.

Silence. The clock struck midnight. A scraping. The door handle slowly turned. *Knock! Knock!* The clock bells rang with a dinging sound. An ear-piercing screech. The door handle rattled. The door shook. Another ear-splitting scream. The wardrobe doors opened. The clothes flew out. The TV screen cracked.

"What do we owe you?" one of the kids asked.

Silence. A maniacal cackle.

"Your lives..."

## Haaris Sarwar (12)
Trinity Academy Grammar, Sowerby Bridge

# THE HUNTER

The hunter opened the creaky door. A shiver went down his spine. He walked into the house, gun shaking viciously. He sighed and started walking up the rusty staircase. He was wondering why he got the job.

Something zoomed past him. He turned around and went to where the door opened. Downstairs the front door slammed shut. The lights turned on.

"Hello?" he questioned.

The lights started flickering and a deathly scream was heard. The gun was now ready to shoot anything, his hand shook over the trigger. He had never been this scared before. Then someone touched his shoulder...

## Annabel Walker (13)
Trinity Academy Grammar, Sowerby Bridge

# THE WOODS

Sunset, in the woods. It was unheard of.

"It's dangerous," they said.

Oh, how I didn't know.

I sneakily crept into the woods. The trees were old and towering. The grass was overgrown. I could swear that something was watching me.

Then I heard, "Help me! Anyone? Help me!"

I was tempted, but I waited.

When it turned around, it was something else. Some of the flesh was rotten and his eyes were red.

He looked at me and shouted, "Please anyone! Help me!"

It knew deep down, it knew. It had found me at last...

## Kamran Azam (13)

Trinity Academy Grammar, Sowerby Bridge

# MAN IN LOS ANGELES

Finally, I arrived in Los Angeles. It was dark, gloomy, and foggy. The fog was as thick as a 'Harry Potter' book. The moon was dimmer than space and it was shivering with fear. There were countless streets and houses. I could see the trees twisting and twirling, trying to reach out to me. I felt petrified.

The thick fog trapped me. Getting ready to devour me. Something stood out to me; a palace peeking above the endless fog. I could hear people screaming for help. As I turned around, I saw a silhouette in the bright light behind...

## Lalith Togalla (13)

Trinity Academy Grammar, Sowerby Bridge

# THE RIPPER

The night was fast approaching. Little Timmy wasn't hungry. He suddenly realised that he had to eat. He was going to have to sleep in five minutes because it was his birthday tomorrow and he couldn't wait. He went to sleep as soon as he could. Little did he know was that would be the last birthday he was going to have.

Timmy woke up. He was bleeding from the stomach. Blood dripped down the bed. He realised he wouldn't be able to celebrate his 9th birthday. He saw his brother staring at him. He felt empty...

## Corbin Taylor (14)
Trinity Academy Grammar, Sowerby Bridge

# DEATH

Rage coursed through my veins. I was trapped! I knew it wasn't on purpose I'd hidden at the back of the horror train ride. I came out from my hiding place. There was nobody nearby.

I walked through the train and saw that all of the horrors were gone, although I hadn't heard anyone moving anything.

When I was in the carriage at the front, I walked in and screamed. There were coffins! I opened one and recognised the face. It was mine! I was dead! I heard a sound behind me. I turned to see Death itself.

## Lily Roberts (13)

Trinity Academy Grammar, Sowerby Bridge

# SATAN

*Splash!* A body was dumped in the North Lake.
The next morning was a hectic one. The police found the
body in a shrivelled up bag. As they opened it slowly, they
got a strong scent of smoke and a smell of damp. As they
pulled the body out, they saw a scorched upside-down cross
on his forehead. As it met direct sunlight, its eyes opened
with a bloodshot colour. His hands jolted up and plunged
into the chests of the officers and ripped their hearts out.
Then it disappeared into a blazing hellish fire.

## Malachy Burns (15)
Trinity Academy Grammar, Sowerby Bridge

# DARKER THAN NIGHT

As I walked through the forest, the gloomy bushy trees surrounded me. All of a sudden, I felt a cold breeze rinse through my body.

As I went deeper into the forest, I could hear the loud rustling of the bushes. Suddenly, in the corner of my eye, I saw a shadow darker than the night sky. Out of nowhere, my foot got stuck in a piece of string. I heard an evil laugh. My heart sunk. I tried to run but it was too late. A tall man had already grabbed the back of my head.

## Nimrah Nabeel (12)
Trinity Academy Grammar, Sowerby Bridge

# THE THREE CURSES

One day, Esther arrived at the orphanage after her parents had died. She met Isaac and Molly. After that, they reserved some toys; a panda, a bunny and a tiger. The bunny and tiger were called Mr Bop and Mr Stripes.

One night, Esther put Mr Bop next to her bed. The next minute he had gone. Mr Bop went to Isaac and Molly's bed and kidnapped and killed them.

As for Esther, her soul and Mr Bop's soul stayed bonded forever...

## Sophie Calder (13)
Trinity Academy Grammar, Sowerby Bridge

# THE DELUSIONAL DETECTIVE

Just a normal day at work. A 'normal' day. I got out of my bed, walked down a dark grimy corridor, grabbing a glock 17 and stepped outside, got in my car and drove to work. "Hey, we need you. A girl, about 6-7 years old, beaten brutally. We need you to go in and talk to him. His name's James."
I walked to the interrogation room.
"Alright James, what's your excuse?"
"I shouldn't be he... Wait. You're the guy who's stuck in his own mind, making up these situations..."
I woke up in my cell.
Help me. You must.

**Josh Torney (14)**
Workington Academy, Workington

# THE ABANDONED FACTORY

*It's our turn to die.* This was my most prominent thought as the ghost hunters advanced towards the metal door of the factory reading: 'Do not enter!' Our hearts raced as we decided to continue into the unknown abyss.

Suddenly, a clatter came from the wreck in front of us. We gathered up courage as we should be experts.

After a while of searching and encountering horrific spiders, our ghost radar beeped frantically. Before we knew what was going on, Joe was lunged into a meat grinder that was roaring like a lion.

Weeks later, everyone had disappeared.

## Acacia McLean (14)
Workington Academy, Workington

# THE LOOP

*Boom!* They knocked her out. She suddenly awoke in an enclosed room with flashing red lights. She decided not to panic and wait to see if someone would give her a visit. Through a speaker in the centre of the room echoed a voice, "You're forever trapped in my loop."

She pondered over what she should do. A group of armed forces charged in and the battle commenced. Everyone threw punches. She was outnumbered. *Boom!* They knocked her out.

She woke up in a red room.

"You're forever trapped in my loop," echoed an eerie voice.

**Jayden Messenger (14)**
Workington Academy, Workington

# LATE HOME

It was midnight... I was supposed to be home. There was an abandoned building next to me. I'll just tell Mum I'm staying out. I rang Mum.

"I'm staying out."

"Okay, hun."

As I walked towards the building, I could feel in my stomach that this was a bad idea.

I stepped inside. I could hear a whimper of noise and felt someone rush past me. I was terrified. I went to turn around to run home but the doors slammed in my face. I tried to call Mum but my phone died.

I called out, "Hello?"

No response...

**Lilly Fidoe (12)**
Workington Academy, Workington

# YOU CANNOT BEAT DEATH

I arrived when the night was cold. It was just like his heart. The lightning struck. It terrified me. He just stood there, careless, with no expression. He was completely heartless, selfish. I don't know who, or even what, it was. It sent shivers down my spine. A voice in my head was telling me to approach, but that would be suicide. Either way, the outcome wasn't good. I could never have won this brawl of emotion. I contemplated challenging it, but it was too late. They were malicious, bloodthirsty, and the traits that really caused my death.

## Preston Keeler (14)
Workington Academy, Workington

# THE FIGURE

Suddenly, my engine stopped. I had to find help. The weather was awful but I couldn't sit in my car forever. Reluctantly, I wandered into the woods, hoping to find someone.

After searching for fifteen minutes, I saw a home. It was at least 100 years old. The rain got much heavier. I sprinted as hastily as I could.

"Is anyone home?" I shouted.

There was no reply. I assumed it was abandoned. There were two thumps. I hid in a closet. A figure entered the room and stared at me.

It whispered, "I see you..."

## Riley McLuckie (14)
Workington Academy, Workington

# THE HOUSE

I was shaking as I got out of the car. I slowly approached the house as the car drove away, headlights going down the road.

I opened the door and it creaked. I walked up the stairs, each footstep sounding like an elephant's. I heard a woman shriek like a banshee. I knew I had to leave.

I tried to walk back down the stairs to get to the door. *Bang!* The doors slammed shut. There were more shrieks. I pulled my absolute hardest at the doors but nothing happened.

A man appeared in front of me.

"Help me..."

**Archie Mahone**
Workington Academy, Workington

# THE KNIFE

One day in one of the most haunted places in England, the Lonely Manor, three young friends went to investigate what really happened at this haunted hotel. There had been hundreds of accidents at this once great hotel.

As soon as they got there, they saw the paranormal activity. Out of nowhere, a knife flew across the room into the wall across the other side of the room. When they pulled it out, they saw blood all over the knife.

Soon after, they set up the equipment and left for dinner. When they came back they were shocked...

## Daniel Weightman (12)
Workington Academy, Workington

# THE NIGHT THE DEAD BECAME THE LIVING

It was just a normal day until my friend and I decided to enter the deserted building. The one where football legend, Phill Foden died in.

My friend, Jackson, thought it would be a good idea to dash his football towards the house. The ball smashed through the second storey window. He decided we should go retrieve it.

We opened the door and peered around the ancient walls that hadn't been seen for many years.

At the top of the stairs, stood a ghostly figure dressed from head toe in an England strip from decades ago...

**Owain Graham (14)**
Workington Academy, Workington

# CREAKY FLOORBOARD

She screamed!
A look of terror came over her face. She quietly walked into the mansion. It was a mess. Scared, she walked into what looked like the old dining room and saw cups of tea being lifted, but nobody was there. She held her breath and backed out of the room.
The next room she walked into looked like a library. She sat down, then a book popped out, and then a door opened. She suddenly felt a sharp scratch down her back.
She tried to run but couldn't. She was dragged back into the dark cupboard...

## Niamh McNicholas (12)
Workington Academy, Workington

# SWEET DREAMS

One day, Adam and some of his friends were at a house playing Truth or Dare.

Ria asked Jay, "Truth or dare?"

Jay replied, "Dare."

His dare was to scare Adam when he went to sleep later on.

A couple of hours went by and it was dark and stormy outside. Kai and Jay asked if they could sleep for the night. He said they could stay.

Later on, there was a strange knocking on the window. Kai, Jay, and Adam woke up to a man standing over them. Kai tried to move but he couldn't...

## Riley Underwood (12)
Workington Academy, Workington

# THE HOUSE

I was there, stood outside the home. It was calling for me to go inside. I walked up the cracked driveway and opened the door with not a single peep. Something was leading me by the hand upstairs. Despite the loud noises, I couldn't stop. The floorboards creaked and lightning struck the abandoned home but I just carried on.

I got to the old closet and suddenly felt a hand shaking my shoulder. It turned out it was my friend, Ben. Neither he nor I knew what it was dragging us into the house.

**Chloe Ellwood (14)**
Workington Academy, Workington

**YoungWriters**® — Est. 1991 —

# YOUNG WRITERS INFORMATION

We hope you have enjoyed reading this book – and that you will continue to in the coming years.

If you're a young writer who enjoys reading and creative writing, or the parent of an enthusiastic poet or story writer, visit our website **www.youngwriters.co.uk/subscribe** to join the World of Young Writers and receive news, competitions, writing challenges, tips, articles and giveaways! There is lots to keep budding writers motivated to write!

If you would like to order further copies of this book, or any of our other titles, then please give us a call or order via your online account.

Young Writers
Remus House
Coltsfoot Drive
Peterborough
PE2 9BF
(01733) 890066
**info@youngwriters.co.uk**

Join in the conversation!
Tips, news, giveaways and much more!

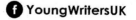 YoungWritersUK    YoungWritersCW   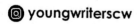 youngwriterscw